HORRID HENRY'S BiG BAD BOOK

FRANCESCA SIMON

HORRiD HENRY'S BiG BAD BOOK

Illustrated by Tony Ross

Orion
Children's Books

First published in Great Britain in 2004
by Orion Children's Books
a division of the Orion Publishing Group Ltd
Orion House
5 Upper Saint Martin's Lane
London WC2H 9EA

5 7 9 10 8 6

A catalogue record for this book is available
from the British Library.

ISBN-13: 978 1 84255 502 6

Printed in Italy

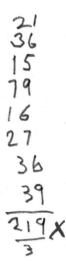

www.orionbooks.co.uk

CONTENTS

Bert   susan   Violet   Kate   Jim   Jac

Henry   Andrew   Brian   Gurinder   Dave   Ralph

HORRID HENRY'S CLASS

oby Zoe Nick Fiona Bob Soraya

Graham Margaret William Clare Linda Al

HORRID HENRY'S NEW TEACHER

'**N**ow Henry,' said Dad. 'Today is the first day of school. A chance for a fresh start with a new teacher.'

'Yeah, yeah,' scowled Horrid Henry.

He hated the first day of term. Another year, another teacher to show who was boss. His first teacher, Miss Marvel, had run screaming from the classroom after two weeks. His next teacher, Mrs Zip, had run screaming from the classroom after one day. Breaking in new teachers wasn't easy, thought Henry, but someone had to do it.

Dad got out a piece of paper and waved it.

'Henry, I never want to read another school report like this again,' he said. 'Why can't your school reports be like Peter's?'

Henry started whistling.

'Pay attention, Henry,' shouted Dad. 'This is important. Look at this report.'

HENRY'S SCHOOL REPORT

It has been horrible Teaching Henry this year. He is rude, lazy and disruptive. The worst student I have ever taught.

Behaviour: Horrid

English: Horrid

Maths: Horrid

Science: Horrid

P.E: Horrid

'What about *my* report?' said Perfect Peter.

Dad beamed.

'Your report was perfect, Peter,' said Dad. 'Keep up the wonderful work.'

PETER'S SCHOOL REPORT

It has been a pleasure teaching Peter this year. He is polite, hard-working and co-operative. The best student I have ever taught.

Behaviour: Perfect

English: Perfect

Maths: Perfect

Science: Perfect

P.E: Perfect

Peter smiled proudly.

'You'll just have to try harder, Henry,' said Peter, smirking.

Horrid Henry was a shark sinking his teeth into a drowning sailor.

'OWWWW,' shrieked Peter. 'Henry bit me!'

'Don't be horrid, Henry!' shouted Dad. 'Or no TV for a week.'

'I don't care,' muttered Henry. When he became king he'd make it a law that parents, not children, had to go to school.

Horrid Henry pushed and shoved his way into class and grabbed the seat next to Rude Ralph.

'Nah nah ne nah nah, I've got a new football,' said Ralph.

Henry didn't have a football. He'd kicked his through Moody Margaret's window.

'Who cares?' said Horrid Henry.

The classroom door slammed. It was Mr Nerdon, the toughest, meanest, nastiest teacher in the school.

'SILENCE!' he said, glaring at them with his bulging eyes. 'I don't want to hear a sound. I don't even want to hear anyone breathe.'

The class held its breath.

'GOOD!' he growled. 'I'm Mr Nerdon.'

Henry snorted. What a stupid name.

'Nerd,' he whispered to Ralph.

Rude Ralph giggled.

'Nerdy Nerd,' whispered Horrid Henry, snickering.

Mr Nerdon walked up to Henry and jabbed his finger in his face.

'Quiet, you horrible boy!' said Mr Nerdon. 'I've got my eye on you. Oh yes. I've heard about your other teachers. Bah! I'm made of stronger stuff. There will be no nonsense in *my* class.'

We'll see about that, thought Henry.

'Our first sums for the year are on the board. Now get to work,' ordered Mr Nerdon.

Horrid Henry had an idea.

Quickly he scribbled a note to Ralph.

Ralph – I bet you that I can make Mr. Nerdon run screaming out of class by the end of lunchtime.

No way, Henry

If I do will you give me your new football?

O.K. But if you don't, you have to give me your pound coin.

O.K.

Horrid Henry took a deep breath and went to work. He rolled up some paper, stuffed it in his mouth, and spat it out. The spitball whizzed through the air and pinged Mr Nerdon on the back of his neck.

Mr Nerdon wheeled round.

'You!' snapped Mr Nerdon. 'Don't you mess with me!'

'It wasn't *me!*' said Henry. 'It was Ralph.'

'Liar!' said Mr Nerdon. 'Sit at the back of the class.'

Horrid Henry moved his seat next to Clever Clare.

'Move over, Henry!' hissed Clare. 'You're on my side of the desk.'

Henry shoved her.

'Move over yourself,' he hissed back.

Then Horrid Henry reached over and broke Clare's pencil.

'Henry broke my pencil!' shrieked Clare.

Mr Nerdon moved Henry next to Weepy William.

Henry pinched him.

Mr Nerdon moved Henry next to Tough Toby.

Henry jiggled the desk.

Mr Nerdon moved Henry next to Lazy Linda.

Henry scribbled all over her paper.

Mr Nerdon moved Henry next to Moody Margaret.

Moody Margaret drew a line down the middle of the desk.

'Cross that line, Henry, and you're dead,' said Margaret under her breath.

Henry looked up. Mr Nerdon was writing spelling words on the board.

Henry started to rub out Margaret's line.

'Stop it, Henry,' said Mr Nerdon, without turning around.

Henry stopped.

Mr Nerdon continued writing.

Henry pulled Margaret's hair.

Mr Nerdon moved Henry next to Beefy Bert, the biggest boy in the class.

Beefy Bert was chewing his pencil and trying to add 2 + 2 without much luck.

Horrid Henry inched his chair onto Beefy Bert's side of the desk.

Bert ignored him.

Henry poked him.
Bert ignored him.
Henry hit him.
POW!
The next thing
Henry knew
he was lying
on the floor,
looking up at
the ceiling.
Beefy Bert
continued chewing his pencil.

'What happened, Bert?' said Mr Nerdon.

'I dunno,' said Beefy Bert.

'Get up off the floor, Henry!' said Mr Nerdon.
A faint smile appeared on the
teacher's slimy lips.

'He hit me!' said
Henry. He'd
never
felt such
a punch
in his life.

'It was an accident,' said Mr Nerdon. He smirked. 'You'll sit next to Bert from now on.'

That's it, thought Henry. Now it's war.

'How absurd, to be a nerdy bird,' said Horrid Henry behind Mr Nerdon's back.

Slowly Mr Nerdon turned and walked towards him. His hand was clenched into a fist.

'Since you're so good at rhyming,' said Mr Nerdon, 'everyone write a poem. Now.'

Henry slumped in his seat and groaned. A poem! Yuck! He hated poems. Even the word *poem* made him want to throw up.

Horrid Henry caught Rude Ralph's eye. Ralph was grinning and mouthing, 'A pound, a pound!' at him. Time was running out. Despite Henry's best efforts, Mr Nerdon still hadn't run screaming from the class. Henry would have to act fast to get that football.

What horrible poem could he write? Horrid Henry smiled. Quickly he picked up his pencil and went to work.

'Now, who's my first victim?' said Mr Nerdon. He looked round the room. 'Susan! Read your poem.'

Sour Susan stood up and read:

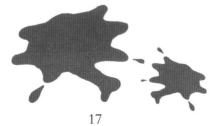

'Bow wow
Bow wow
Woof woof woof
I'm a dog, not a cat, so...
SCAT!'

'Not enough rhymes,' said Mr Nerdon. 'Next…' He looked round the room. 'Graham!'

Greedy Graham stood up and read:

'Chocolate chocolate chocolate sweet,
Cakes and doughnuts can't be beat.
Ice cream is my favourite treat
With lots and lots of pie to eat!'

'Too many rhymes,' said Mr Nerdon. 'Next…' He scowled at the class. Henry tried to look as if he didn't want the teacher to call on him.

'Henry!' snapped Mr Nerdon. 'Read your poem!'

Horrid Henry stood up and read:

'Pirates puke on stormy seas,
Giants spew on top of trees.'

Henry peeked at Mr Nerdon. He looked pale. Henry continued to read:

'Kings are sick in golden loos,
Dogs throw up on Daddy's shoes.'

Henry peeked again at Mr Nerdon. He
looked green. Any minute now, thought
Henry, and he'll be out of here screaming.
He read on:

'Babies love to make a mess,
Down the front of Mum's best dress,
And what car ride would be complete,
Without the stink of last night's treat?'

'That's enough,' choked Mr Nerdon.
'Wait, I haven't got to the good bit,' said Horrid
Henry.
'I said that's enough!' gasped Mr Nerdon. 'You fail.'
He made a big black mark in his book.
'I threw up on the boat!' shouted Greedy Graham.
'I threw up on the plane!' shouted Sour Susan.
'I threw up in the car!' shouted Dizzy Dave.
'I said that's enough!' ordered Mr Nerdon. He glared
at Horrid Henry. 'Get out of here, all of you! It's
lunchtime.'
Rats, thought Henry. Mr Nerdon was one tough
teacher.

Rude Ralph grabbed him.

'Ha ha, Henry,' said Ralph. 'You lose. Gimme that pound.'

'No,' said Henry. 'I've got until the end of lunch.'

'You can't do anything to him between now and then,' said Ralph.

'Oh yeah?' said Henry. 'Just watch me.'

Then Henry had a wonderful, spectacular idea. This was it. The best plan he'd ever had. Someday someone would stick a plaque on the school wall celebrating Henry's genius. There would be songs written about him. He'd probably even get a medal. But first things first. In order for his plan to work to perfection, he needed Peter.

Perfect Peter was playing hopscotch with his friends Tidy Ted and Spotless Sam.

'Hey Peter,' said Henry. 'How would you like to be a real member of the Purple Hand?'

The Purple Hand was Horrid Henry's secret club. Peter had wanted to join for ages, but naturally Henry would never let him.

Peter's jaw dropped open.

'Me?' said Peter.

'Yes,' said Henry. 'If you can pass the secret club test.'

'What do I have to do?' said Peter eagerly.

'It's tricky,' said Henry. 'And probably much too hard for you.'

'Tell me, tell me,' said Peter.

'All you have to do is lie down right there below that window and stay absolutely still. You mustn't move until I tell you to.'

'Why?' said Peter.

'Because that's the test,' said Henry.

Perfect Peter thought for a moment.

'Are you going to drop something on me?'

'No,' said Henry.

'OK,' said Peter. He lay down obediently.

'And I need your shoes,' said Henry.

'Why?' said Peter.

Henry scowled.

'Do you want to be in the Purple Hand or not?' said Henry.

'I do,' said Peter.

'Then give me your shoes and be quiet,' said Henry. 'I'll be checking on you. If I see you moving one little bit you can't be in my club.'

Peter gave Henry his trainers, then lay still as a statue.

Horrid Henry grabbed the shoes, then dashed up the stairs to his classroom.

It was empty. Good.

Horrid Henry went over to the window and opened it. Then he stood there, holding one of Peter's shoes in each hand.

Henry waited until he heard Mr Nerdon's footsteps. Then he went into action.

'Help!' shouted Horrid Henry. 'Help!'

Mr Nerdon entered. He saw Henry and glowered.

'What are you doing here? Get out!'

'Help!' shouted Henry. 'I can't hold on to him much longer… he's slipping… aaahhh, he's fallen!'

Horrid Henry held up the empty shoes.

'He's gone,' whispered Henry. He peeked out of the window. 'Ugghh, I can't look.'

Mr Nerdon went pale. He ran to the window and saw Perfect Peter lying still and shoeless on the ground below.

'Oh no,' gasped Mr Nerdon.

'I'm sorry,' panted Henry. 'I tried to hold on to him, honest, I –'

'Help!' screamed Mr Nerdon. He raced down the stairs. 'Police! Fire! Ambulance! Help! Help!'

He ran over to Peter and knelt by his still body.

'Can I get up now, Henry?' said Perfect Peter.

'What!?' gasped Mr Nerdon. 'What did you say?'

Then the terrible truth dawned. He, Ninius Nerdon, had been tricked.

'YOU HORRID BOY! GO STRAIGHT TO THE HEAD TEACHER – NOW!' screeched Mr Nerdon.

Perfect Peter jumped to his feet.

'But... but –' spluttered Perfect Peter.

'Now!' screamed Mr Nerdon. 'How dare you! To the head!'

'AAAGGGHHHH,' shrieked Peter.

He slunk off to the head's office, weeping.

Mr Nerdon turned to race up the stairs to grab Henry.

'I'll get you, Henry!' he screamed. His face was white. He looked as if he were going to faint.

'Help,' squeaked Mr Nerdon.
Then he fainted.

Clunk! Thunk! Thud!
NEE NAW NEE NAW NEE NAW.
When the ambulance arrived, the only person lying on the ground was Mr Nerdon. They scooped him on to a stretcher and took him away.

The perfect end to a perfect day, thought Horrid Henry, throwing his new football in the air. Peter sent home in disgrace. Mr Nerdon gone for good. Even the news that scary Miss Battle-Axe would be teaching Henry's class didn't bother him. After all, tomorrow was another day.

HORRID HENRY'S FAVOURITE POEM

I'm Gonna Throw Up

Pirates puke on stormy seas
Giants spew on top of trees.
Kings are sick in golden loos
Dogs throw up on Daddy's shoes.

Babies love to make a mess
Down the front of Mum's best dress.
And what car ride would be complete
Without the stink of last night's treat?

Teachers who force kids to eat
Shepherd's pie with rancid meat
Can't be surprised when at their feet
The upchucked meal splats complete.

Rollercoasters, swirling cups
Can make anyone throw up.
Ferris wheels, icky sweets,
Pavement pizzas spray the streets.

Hats are handy when in town
Should your guts flip upside down.
A bag's a fine and private place
To avoid public disgrace
When, tummy heaving, insides peeling,
You suddenly get that awful feeling —
'Mum! I'm gonna throw up!'

If you're caught short while at sea
Don't worry! You'll die eventually.
But I for one do not believe
That bobbing ships cause folk to heave.
Sitting at the Captain's table
I scoffed as much as I was able.
I ate so many lovely dishes —
URGHHH! Now it's time to feed
the fishes.

HORRID HENRY'S NITS

Scratch. Scratch. Scratch.

Dad scratched his head.

'Stop scratching, please,' said Mum. 'We're eating dinner.'

Mum scratched her head.

'Stop scratching, please,' said Dad. 'We're eating dinner.'

Henry scratched his head.

'Stop scratching, Henry!' said Mum and Dad.

'Uh-oh,' said Mum. She put down her fork and frowned at Henry.

'Henry, do you have nits *again*?'

'Of course not,' said Henry.

'Come over to the sink, Henry,' said Mum.

'Why?' said Henry.

'I need to check your head.'

Henry dragged his feet over to her as slowly as possible. It's not fair, he thought. It wasn't his fault nits loved him. Henry's head was a gathering place for nits far and wide. They probably held nit parties there and foreign nits visited him on their holidays.

Mum dragged the nit comb across Henry's head. She made a face and groaned.

'You're crawling with nits, Henry,' said Mum.

'Ooh, let's see,' said Henry. He always liked counting how many nits he had.

'One, two, three ... forty-five, forty-six, forty-seven ...' he counted, dropping them on to a paper towel.

'It's not polite to count nits,' said his younger brother, Perfect Peter, wiping his mouth with his spotless napkin, 'is it, Mum?'

'It certainly isn't,' said Mum.

Dad dragged the nit comb across his head and made a face.

'Ughh,' said Dad.

Mum dragged the comb through her hair.

'Bleeeech,' said Mum.

Mum combed Perfect Peter's hair. Then she did it again. And again. And again.

'No nits, Peter,' said Mum, smiling. 'As usual. Well done, darling.'

Perfect Peter smiled modestly.

'It's because I wash and comb my hair every night,' said Peter.

Henry scowled. True, his hair was filthy, but then ...

'Nits love clean hair,' said Henry.

'No they don't,' said Peter. '*I've* never ever had nits.'

We'll see about that, thought Henry. When no one was looking he picked a few nits off the paper towel. Then he wandered over to Peter and casually fingered a lock of his hair.

LEAP!

Scratch. Scratch.

'Mum!' squealed Peter. 'Henry's pulling my hair!'

'Stop it, Henry,' said Dad.

'I wasn't pulling his hair,' said Henry indignantly. 'I just wanted to see how clean it was. And it is so lovely and clean,' added Henry sweetly. 'I wish my hair was as clean as Peter's.'

Peter beamed. It wasn't often that Henry said anything nice to him.

'Right,' said Mum grimly, 'everyone upstairs. It's shampoo time.'

'NO!' shrieked Horrid Henry.

'NO SHAMPOO!'

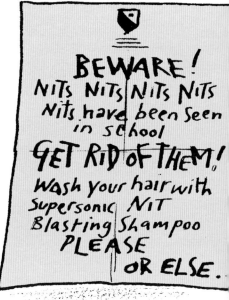

He hated the stinky smelly horrible shampoo much more than he hated having nits. Only today his teacher, Miss Battle-Axe, had sent home a nit letter.

Naturally, Henry had crumpled up the letter and thrown it away. He was never ever going to have pongy nit shampoo on his head again. What rotten luck Mum had spotted him scratching.

'It's the only way to get rid of nits,' said Dad.

'But it never works!' screamed Henry. And he ran for the door.

Mum and Dad grabbed him. Then they dragged him kicking and screaming to the bathroom.

'Nits are living creatures,' howled Henry. 'Why kill them?'

'Because . . .' said Mum.

'Because . . . because . . . they're blood-sucking nits,' said Dad.

Blood-sucking. Henry had never thought of that. In the split second that he stood still to consider this interesting information, Mum emptied the bottle of supersonic nit-blasting shampoo over his hair.

'NO!' screamed Henry.

Frantically he shook his head. There was shampoo on the door. There was shampoo on the floor. There was shampoo all over Mum and Dad. The only place there was no shampoo was on Henry's head.

'Henry! Stop being horrid!' yelled Dad, wiping shampoo off his shirt.

'What a big fuss over nothing,' said Peter.

Henry lunged at him. Mum seized Henry by the collar and held him back.

'Now Peter,' said Mum. 'That wasn't a kind thing to say to Henry, was it? Not everyone is as brave as you.'

'You're right, Mum,' said Perfect Peter. 'I was being rude and thoughtless. It won't happen again. I'm so sorry, Henry.'

Mum smiled at him. 'That was a perfect apology, Peter. As for you, Henry . . .' she sighed. 'We'll get more shampoo tomorrow.'

Phew, thought Henry, giving his head an extra good scratch. Safe for one more day.

The next morning at school a group of parents burst into the classroom, waving the nit letter and shouting.

'My Margaret doesn't have nits!' shrieked Moody

Margaret's mother. 'She never has and she never will. How dare you send home such a letter!'

'My Josh doesn't have nits,' shouted his mother. 'The idea!'

'My Toby doesn't have nits!' shouted his father. 'Some nasty child in this class isn't bug-busting!'

Miss Battle-Axe squared her shoulders.

'Rest assured that the culprit will be found,' she said. 'I have declared war on nits.'

Scratch. Scratch. Scratch.

Miss Battle-Axe spun round. Her beady eyes swivelled over the class.

'Who's scratching?' she demanded.

Silence.

Henry bent over his worksheet and tried to look studious.

'Henry is,' said Moody Margaret.

'Liar!' shouted Horrid Henry. 'It was William!'

Weepy William burst into tears.

'No it wasn't,' he sobbed.

Miss Battle-Axe glared at the class.

'I'm going to find out once and for all who's got nits,' she growled.

'I don't!' shouted Moody Margaret.

'I don't!' shouted Rude Ralph.

'I don't!' shouted Horrid Henry.

'Silence!' ordered Miss Battle-Axe. 'Nora, the nit nurse, is coming this morning. Who's got nits? Who's not bug-busting? We'll all find out soon.'

Uh-oh, thought Henry. Now I'm sunk. There was no escaping Nitty Nora Bug Explorer and her ferocious combs. Everyone would know *he* had the nits. Rude Ralph would never stop teasing him. He'd be shampooed every night. Mum and Dad would find out about all the nit letters he'd thrown away . . .

He could of course get a tummy ache double quick and be sent home. But Nitty Nora had a horrible way of remembering whose head she hadn't checked and then combing it in front of the whole class.

He could run screaming out of the door saying he'd caught mad cow disease. But somehow he didn't think Miss Battle-Axe would believe him.

There was no way out. This time he was well and truly stuck.

Unless . . .

Suddenly Henry had a wonderful, spectacular idea. It was so wicked, and so horrible, that even Horrid Henry hesitated. But only for a moment. Desperate times call for desperate measures.

Henry leaned over Clever Clare and brushed his head lightly against hers.

LEAP!

Scratch. Scratch.

'Get away from me, Henry,' hissed Clare.

'I was just admiring your lovely picture,' said Henry.

He got up to sharpen his pencil. On his way to the sharpener he brushed against Greedy Graham.

LEAP!

Scratch. Scratch.

On his way back from the sharpener Henry stumbled and fell against Anxious Andrew.

LEAP!

Scratch. Scratch.

'Ow!' yelped Andrew.

'Sorry, Andrew,' said Henry. 'What big clumsy feet I have. Whoops!' he added, tripping over the carpet and banging heads with Weepy William.

LEAP!

Scratch. Scratch.

'Waaaaaaaaa!' wailed William.

'Sit down at once, Henry,' said Miss Battle-Axe. 'William! Stop scratching. Bert! How do you spell cat?'

'I dunno,' said Beefy Bert.

Horrid Henry leaned across the table and put his head close to Bert's.

'C-A-T,' he whispered helpfully.

LEAP!

Scratch. Scratch.

Then Horrid Henry raised his hand.

'Yes?' said Miss Battle-Axe.

'I don't understand these instructions,' said Henry sweetly. 'Could you help me, please?'

Miss Battle-Axe frowned. She liked to keep as far away from Henry as possible. Reluctantly she came closer and bent over his work. Henry leaned his head near hers.

LEAP!

Scratch. Scratch.

There was a pounding at the door. Then Nitty Nora marched into the classroom, bristling with combs and other instruments of torture.

'Line up, everyone,' said Miss Battle-Axe, patting her hair. 'The nit nurse is here.'

Rats, thought Henry. He'd hardly started. Slowly he stood up.

Everyone pushed and shoved to be first in line. Then a few children remembered what they were lining up for and stampeded towards the back. Horrid Henry saw his chance and took it.

He charged through the squabbling children, brushing against everyone as fast as he could.

Scratch! Scratch! LEAP!

Scratch! Scratch! LEAP!

Scratch! Scratch! LEAP!

'Henry!' shouted Miss Battle-Axe. 'Stay in at playtime. Now go to the end of the queue. The rest of you, stop this nonsense at once!'

Moody Margaret had fought longest and hardest to be first. Proudly she presented her head to Nitty Nora.

'I certainly don't have nits,' she said.

Nitty Nora stuck the comb in.

'Nits!' she announced, stuffing a nit note into Margaret's hand.

For once Margaret was too shocked to speak.

'But ... but ...' she gasped.

Tee-hee, thought Henry. Now he wouldn't be the only one.

'Next,' said Nitty Nora.

She stuck the comb in Rude Ralph's greasy hair.

'Nits!' she announced.

'Nit-face,' hissed Horrid Henry, beside himself with glee.

'Nits!' said Nitty Nora, poking her comb into Lazy Linda's mop.

'Nits!' said Nitty Nora, prodding Greedy Graham's frizzy hair.

'Nits, nits, nits, nits, nits!' she continued, pointing at

Weepy William, Clever Clare, Sour Susan, Beefy Bert and Dizzy Dave.

Then Nitty Nora beckoned to Miss Battle-Axe.

'Teachers too,' she ordered.

Miss Battle-Axe's jaw dropped.

'I have been teaching for twenty- five years and I have never had nits,' she said. 'Don't waste your time checking *me*.'

Nitty Nora ignored her protests and stuck in the comb.

'Hmmn,' she said, and whispered in Miss Battle-Axe's ear.

'NO!' howled Miss Battle-Axe. 'NOOOOOOOO!' Then she joined the line of weeping, wailing children clutching their nit notes.

At last it was Henry's turn.

Nitty Nora stuck her comb into Henry's tangled hair

39

and dragged it along his scalp. She combed again. And again. And again.

'No nits,' said Nitty Nora. 'Keep up the good work, young man.'

'I sure will!' said Henry.

Horrid Henry skipped home waving his certificate.

'Look, Peter,' crowed Henry. 'I'm nit-free!'

Perfect Peter burst into tears.

'I'm not,' he wailed.

'Hard luck,' said Horrid Henry.

Margaret has nits! pass it on
Henry wears nappies! pass it on
Margaret is a nit-face
Henry needs his nappy changed
Nitty
Smelly

HORRID HENRY'S
SCHOOL TRIP

'Don't forget my packed lunch for the school trip,' shouted Horrid Henry for the tenth time.

'I want crisps, biscuits, chocolate, and a fizzywizz drink.'

'No way, Henry,' said Dad grimly, slicing carrots. 'I'm making you a healthy, nutritious lunch.'

'But I don't want a healthy lunch,' howled Henry. 'I like sweets!'

'Sweets, yuck,' said Perfect Peter. He peeked in his lunch box.

'Oh boy, an apple!' said Peter. 'And egg and cress on brown bread with the crusts on! And carrot and celery sticks, my favourite! Thank you so much, Dad. Henry, if you don't eat healthy food, you'll never grow big and strong.'

'Oh yeah,' said Henry. 'I'll show you how big and strong I am, you little pipsqueak,' he added, springing at Peter. He was a boa constrictor throttling his prey.

'Uggghhhh,' choked Peter.

'Stop being horrid, Henry!' shouted Mum. 'Or there will be no school trip for you.'

Henry let Peter go. Horrid Henry loved school trips. No work. No assembly. A packed lunch. A chance to fool around all day. What could be better?

'I'm going to the Frosty Freeze Ice Cream factory,' said Henry. 'Free ice creams for everyone. Yippee!'

Perfect Peter made a face. 'I don't like ice cream,' he

said. 'My class is going somewhere much better – our Town Museum. And Mum's coming to help.'

'I'd rather be boiled alive and eaten by cannibals than go to that boring old dump,' said Horrid Henry, shuddering. Mum had dragged him there once. Never again.

Then Henry noticed Peter's T-shirt. It was exactly the same as his, purple striped with gold stars.

'Tell Peter to stop copying what I wear to school!' screamed Henry.

'It doesn't matter, Henry,' said Mum. 'You're going on different trips. No one will notice.'

'Just keep out of my way, Peter,' snarled Henry. 'I don't want anyone to think we're related.'

Horrid Henry's class buzzed with excitement as they scrambled to be first on the bus.

'I've got crisps!' shouted Dizzy Dave.

'I've got biscuits!' shouted Anxious Andrew.

'I've got toffee and chocolate and lollies and three fizzywizzes!' shouted Greedy Graham.

'WAAAA,' wailed Weepy William. 'I forgot my packed lunch.'

'Quiet!' ordered Miss Battle-Axe as the bus started moving. 'Sit still and behave. No eating on the bus. William, stop weeping.'

'I need a wee!' shouted Lazy Linda.

'Well, you'll have to wait,' snapped Miss Battle-Axe.

Horrid Henry had trampled his way to the window seats at the back next to Rude Ralph and Greedy Graham. He liked those seats best. Miss Battle-Axe couldn't see him, and he could make faces at all the people in the cars behind him.

Henry and Ralph rolled down the window and chanted:

'Beans, beans, good for the heart,

The more you eat, the more you –'

'HENRY!' bellowed Miss Battle-Axe. 'Turn around and face forward NOW!'

'I need a wee!' shouted Dizzy Dave.

'Look what I've got, Henry,' said Greedy Graham, holding a bulging bag of sweets.

'Gimme some,' said Henry.

'And me,' said Rude Ralph.

The three boys stuffed their faces with sweets.

'Ugh, a green lime,' said Henry, taking the sticky

sweet out of his mouth. 'Eeech.' He flicked the sweet away.

PING!

The sweet landed on Moody Margaret's neck.
'Ow,' said Margaret.
She turned round and glared at Henry.
'Stop it, Henry!' she snarled.
'I didn't do anything,' said Henry.

PING!
A sweet landed in Sour Susan's hair.

PING!
A sweet stuck on Anxious Andrew's new jumper.
'Henry's throwing sweets!' shouted Margaret.
Miss Battle-Axe turned round.
'Henry! Sit next to me,' she said.
'I needed a wee!' wailed Weepy William.

Finally, the bus drove up to the Frosty Freeze Factory. A gigantic, delicious-looking ice cream cone loomed above it.

'We're here!' shouted Henry.

'You scream! I scream! We all scream for ice cream!' shrieked the children as the bus stopped outside the gate.

'Why are we waiting here?' yelled Greedy Graham. 'I want my ice creams now!'

Henry stuck his head out of the window. The gates were chained shut. A large sign read: 'CLOSED on Mondays.'

Miss Battle-Axe looked pale. 'I don't believe this,' she muttered.

'Class, there's been a mix-up, and we seem to have come on the wrong day,' said Miss Battle-Axe. 'But never mind. We'll go to –'

'The Science Museum!' shouted Clever Clare.

'The zoo!' shouted Dizzy Dave.

'Lazer Zap!' shouted Horrid Henry.

'No,' said Miss Battle-Axe. 'Our Town Museum.'

'Ugggghhhhh,' groaned the class.

No one groaned louder than Horrid Henry.

The children left their jackets and lunch boxes in the packed lunch room, and then followed the museum guide to Room 1.

'First we'll see Mr Jones's collection of rubber bands,' said the guide. 'Then our famous display of door hinges and dog collars through history. And don't worry, you'll be seeing our latest acquisitions, soil from Miss Montague's garden and the Mayor's baby pictures.'

Horrid Henry had to escape.

'I need a wee,' said Henry.

'Hurry up then,' said Miss Battle-Axe. 'And come straight back.'

The toilets were next to the packed lunch room.

Henry thought he'd make sure his lunch was still there. Yup, there it was, right next to Ralph's.

I wonder what Ralph has got, thought Henry, staring at Ralph's packed lunch. No harm in looking.

WOW. Rude Ralph's lunchbox was bursting with crisps, sweets, and a chocolate spread sandwich on white bread.

He'll feel sick if he eats all that junk food, thought Henry. I'd better help him.

It was the work of a moment to swap Ralph's sandwich for Henry's egg and cress.

This certainly isn't very healthy, thought Henry, gazing at Greedy Graham's goodies. I'll do him a favour and exchange a few of my celery sticks for his sweets.

Just look at all those treats, thought Henry, fingering Sour Susan's cakes. She should eat a more balanced meal.

A pack of raisins zipped from Henry's lunchbox to Susan's and a sticky bun leapt from Susan's to Henry's.

Tsk tsk, thought Henry, helping himself to Tough Toby's chocolate bar and replacing it with an apple. Too many sweets are bad for the teeth.

That's better, he thought, gazing at his re-packed lunch with satisfaction. Then he strolled back to his class, who were gathered round a glass case.

'This is the soil in which Miss Montague grew her prize-winning vegetables,' droned the guide. 'She grew marrows, tomatoes, potatoes, leeks –'

'When do we eat?' interrupted Horrid Henry.

'I'm starving,' whined Greedy Graham.

'My tummy's rumbling,' groaned Rude Ralph.

'When's lunch?' moaned Moody Margaret.

'WE'RE HUNGRY!' wailed the children.

'All right,' said Miss Battle-Axe. 'We'll eat now.'

The class stampeded down the hall and grabbed their lunches. Henry sat in a corner and tucked in.

For a moment there was silence, then the room echoed with howls of dismay.

'Where's my sticky bun?' yelped Sour Susan.

'My sweets are gone!' screamed Greedy Graham.

'What's this? Egg and cress? Yuck!' shouted Rude Ralph, hurling the sandwich at Anxious Andrew.

That did it. The room filled with flying carrot and celery sticks, granola bars, raisins, crusts, and apples. Henry smirked as he wiped the last traces of chocolate from his mouth.

'Stop it! Stop it!' howled Miss Battle-Axe. 'Well done, Henry, for being the only sensible child. You may lead us back to see the pieces of Roman pottery in Room 2.'

Horrid Henry walked proudly at the head of the shuffling, whining children. Then he noticed the lift at the far end. A sign read:

I wonder where that lift goes, thought Horrid Henry.

'Stop him!' yelled a guard.

But it was too late.

Henry had dashed to the lift and pressed the top button.

Up up up he zipped.

Henry found himself in a small room filled with half-finished exhibits. On display were lists of overdue library books, 'lightbulbs from 1965 to today,' and rows and rows of rocks.

Then, in the corner, Henry actually saw something interesting: a dog's skeleton protected by a drooping blue cord.

Henry looked more closely.

It's just a pile of bones, thought Henry.

He wobbled the blue cord then stood on it.

'Look at me, I'm a tightrope walker,' chortled Horrid Henry, swaying on the blue cord. 'I'm the best tightrope walker in – AGGGHHHH!'

Horrid Henry lost his balance and toppled against the skeleton.

CLITTER-CLATTER! The bones crashed to the ground.

DING DING DING. A burglar alarm began to wail.

Museum guards ran into the room.

Uh-oh, thought Horrid Henry. He slipped between a guard's legs and ran. Behind him he could hear pounding feet.

Henry dashed into a large room filled with road signs, used bus tickets and traffic cones. At the other end of the room Henry saw Peter's class gathered in front of 'The Story of the Drain'. Oh no. There was Mum.

Henry ducked behind the traffic cones.
Museum guards entered.

'There he is!' shouted one. 'The boy in the purple
T-shirt with the gold stars.'

Henry stood fixed to the spot. He was trapped. Then
the guards ran straight past his hiding place. A long
arm reached over and plucked Perfect Peter from
his group.

'Come with us, you!' snarled the guard. 'We're going
straight to the Bad Children's Room.'

'But ... but ...' gasped Peter.

'No ifs or buts!' snapped the guard. 'Who's in charge
of this child?'

'I am,' said Mum. 'What's the meaning of this?'

'You come too,' ordered the guard.

'But ... but ...' gasped Mum.

Shouting and protesting, Mum and Perfect Peter
were taken away.

Then Henry heard a familiar booming voice.

'Margaret, that's enough pushing,' said Miss Battle-Axe. 'No touching, Ralph. Stop weeping, William. Hurry up, everyone! The bus leaves in five minutes. Walk quietly to the exit.'

Everyone immediately started running.

Horrid Henry waited until most of the children had charged past then rejoined the group.

'Where have you been, Henry?' snapped Miss Battle-Axe.

'Just enjoying this brilliant museum,' said Horrid Henry. 'When can we come back?'

HORRID HENRY'S WORST TEACHERS

HORRID HENRY'S
SPORTS DAY

'We all want sports day to be a great success tomorrow,' announced Miss Battle-Axe. 'I am here to make sure that *no one*' – she glared at Horrid Henry – 'spoils it.'

Horrid Henry glared back. Horrid Henry hated sports day. Last year he hadn't won a single event. He'd dropped his egg in the egg-and-spoon race, tripped over Rude Ralph in the three-legged race, and collided with Sour Susan in the sack race. Henry's team had even lost the tug-of-war. Most sickening of all, Perfect Peter had won *both* his races.

If only the school had a sensible day, like TV-watching day, or chocolate-eating day, or who could guzzle the most crisps day, Horrid Henry would be sure to win every prize. But no. *He* had to leap and dash about getting hot and bothered in front of stupid parents. When he became king he'd make teachers run all the races then behead the winners. King Henry the Horrible grinned happily.

'Pay attention, Henry!' barked Miss Battle-Axe. 'What did I just say?'

Henry had no idea. 'Sports day is cancelled?' he suggested hopefully.

Miss Battle-Axe fixed him with her steely eyes. 'I said no one is to bring any sweets tomorrow. You'll all be given a delicious, refreshing piece of orange.'

Henry slumped in his chair, scowling. All he could
do was hope for rain.

Sports day dawned bright and sunny. Rats, thought
Henry. He could, of course, pretend to be sick. But he'd
tried that last year and Mum hadn't been fooled. The
year before that he'd complained he'd hurt his leg.
Unfortunately Dad then caught him dancing on the
table.

It was no use. He'd just have to take part. If only he
could win a race!

Perfect Peter bounced into his room.

'Sports day today!' beamed Peter. 'And *I'm*
responsible for bringing the hard-boiled eggs for
the egg-and-spoon races. Isn't it exciting!'

'NO!' screeched Henry. 'Get out of here!'

'But I only …' began Peter.

Henry leapt at
him, roaring. He
was a cowboy
lassoing a
runaway steer.

'Eeeaaargh!'
squealed Peter.

'Stop being horrid, Henry!' shouted Dad. 'Or no pocket money this week!'

Henry let Peter go.

'It's so unfair,' he muttered, picking up his clothes from the floor and putting them on. Why did he never win?

Henry reached under his bed and filled his pockets from the secret sweet tin he kept there. Horrid Henry was a master at eating sweets in school without being detected. At least he could scoff something good while the others were stuck eating dried-up old orange pieces.

Then he stomped downstairs. Perfect Peter was busy packing hard-boiled eggs into a carton.

Horrid Henry sat down scowling and gobbled his breakfast.

'Good luck, boys,' said Mum. 'I'll be there to cheer for you.'

'Humph,' growled Henry.

'Thanks, Mum,' said Peter. 'I expect I'll win my egg-and-spoon race again but of course it doesn't matter if I don't. It's *how* you play that counts.'

'Shut up, Peter!' snarled Henry. Egg-and-spoon! Egg-and-spoon! If Henry heard that disgusting phrase once more he would start frothing at the mouth.

'Mum! Henry told me to shut up,' wailed Peter, 'and he attacked me this morning.'

'Stop being horrid, Henry,' said Mum. 'Peter, come with me and we'll comb your hair. I want you to look your best when you win that trophy again.'

Henry's blood boiled. He felt like snatching those eggs and hurling them against the wall.

Then Henry had a wonderful, spectacular idea. It was so wonderful that … Henry heard Mum coming back down the stairs. There was no time to lose crowing about his brilliance.

Horrid Henry ran to the fridge, grabbed another egg carton and swapped it for the box of hard-boiled ones on the counter.

'Don't forget your eggs, Peter,' said Mum. She handed the carton to Peter, who tucked it safely in his school bag.

Tee hee, thought Horrid Henry.

Henry's class lined up on the playing fields. Flash! A small figure wearing gleaming white trainers zipped by. It was Aerobic Al, the fastest boy in Henry's class.

'Gotta run, gotta run, gotta run,' he chanted, gliding into place beside Henry. 'I will, of course, win every event,' he announced. 'I've been training all year. My dad's got a special place all ready for my trophies.'

'Who wants to race anyway?' sneered Horrid Henry, sneaking a yummy gummy fuzzball into his mouth.

'Now, teams for the three-legged race,' barked Miss Battle-Axe into her megaphone. 'This is a race showing how well you cooperate and use teamwork with your partner. Ralph will race with William, Josh will race with Clare, Henry …' she glanced at her list '… you will race with Margaret.'

'NO!' screamed Horrid Henry.

'NO!' screamed Moody Margaret.

'Yes,' said Miss Battle-Axe.

'But I want to be with Susan,' said Margaret.

'No fussing,' said Miss Battle-Axe. 'Bert, where's your partner?'

'I dunno,' said Beefy Bert.

Henry and Margaret stood as far apart as possible while their legs were tied together.

'You'd better do as I say, Henry,' hissed Margaret. '*I'll* decide how we race.'

'*I* will, you mean,' hissed Henry.

'Ready ... steady ... GO!'

Miss Battle-Axe blew her whistle.

They were off! Henry moved to the left, Margaret moved to the right.

'This way, Henry!' shouted Margaret. She tried to drag him.

'No, this way!' shouted Henry. He tried to drag her.

They lurched wildly, left and right, then toppled over.

CRASH! Aerobic Al and Lazy Linda tripped over the screaming Henry and Margaret.

SMASH! Rude Ralph and Weepy William fell over Al and Linda.

BUMP! Dizzy Dave and Beefy Bert collided with Ralph and William.

'Waaa!' wailed Weepy William.

'It's all your fault, Margaret!' shouted Henry, pulling her hair.

'No, yours,' shouted Margaret, pulling his harder.

Miss Battle-Axe blew her whistle frantically.

'Stop! Stop!' she ordered. 'Henry! Margaret! What an example to set for the younger ones. Any more nonsense like that and you'll be severely punished. Everyone, get ready for the egg-and-spoon race!'

This was it! The moment Henry had been waiting for.

The children lined up in their teams. Moody Margaret, Sour Susan and Anxious Andrew were going

first in Henry's class. Henry glanced at Peter. Yes, there
he was, smiling proudly, next to Goody-Goody Gordon,
Spotless Sam, and Tidy Ted. The eggs lay still on their
spoons. Horrid Henry held his breath.

'Ready ... steady ... GO!' shouted Miss Battle-Axe.
They were off!

'Go, Peter, go!' shouted Mum.

Peter walked faster and faster and faster. He was in
the lead. He was pulling away from the field. Then ...
wobble ... wobble ... SPLAT!

'Aaaaagh!' yelped Peter.

Moody Margaret's egg
wobbled.

SPLAT!

Then Susan's.

SPLAT!

Then everybody's.

SPLAT!

SPLAT!

SPLAT!

'I've got egg
on my shoes!'
wailed Margaret.

'I've ruined my new dress!' shrieked Susan.

'I've got egg all over me!' squealed Tidy Ted.

'Help!' squeaked Perfect Peter. Egg dripped down his
trousers.

Parents surged forward, screaming and waving hand-kerchiefs and towels.

Rude Ralph and Horrid Henry shrieked with laughter.

Miss Battle-Axe blew her whistle.

'Who brought the eggs?' asked Miss Battle-Axe. Her voice was like ice.

'I did,' said Perfect Peter. 'But I brought hard-boiled ones.'

'OUT!' shouted Miss Battle-Axe. 'Out of the games!'

'But … but …' gasped Perfect Peter.

'No buts, out!' she glared. 'Go straight to the Head.'

Perfect Peter burst into tears and crept away.

Horrid Henry could hardly contain himself. This was the best sports day he'd ever been to.

'The rest of you, stop laughing at once. Parents, get back to your seats! Time for the next race!' ordered Miss Battle-Axe.

All things considered, thought Horrid Henry, lining up with his class, it hadn't been too terrible a day. He'd loved the egg-and-spoon race, of course. And he'd had fun pulling the other team into a muddy puddle in the tug-of-war, knocking over the obstacles in the obstacle race, and crashing into Aerobic Al in the sack race. But, oh, to actually win something!

There was just one race left before sports day was over. The cross-country run. The event Henry hated more than any other. One long, sweaty, exhausting lap round the whole field.

Henry heaved his heavy bones to the starting line. His final chance to win … yet he knew there was no hope. If he beat Weepy William he'd be doing well.

Suddenly Henry had a wonderful, spectacular idea. Why had he never thought of this before? Truly, he was a genius. Wasn't there some ancient Greek who'd won a race by throwing down golden apples which his rival kept stopping to pick up? Couldn't he, Henry, learn something from those old Greeks?

'Ready … steady … GO!' shrieked Miss Battle-Axe. Off they dashed.

'Go, Al, go!' yelled his father.

'Get a move on, Margaret!' shrieked her mother.

'Go, Ralph!' cheered his father.

'Do your best, Henry,' said Mum.

Horrid Henry reached into his pocket and hurled some sweets. They thudded to the ground in front of the runners.

'Look, sweets!' shouted Henry.

Al checked behind him. He was well in the lead. He paused and scooped up one sweet, and then another. He glanced behind again, then started unwrapping the yummy gummy fuzzball.

'Sweets!' yelped Greedy Graham. He stopped to pick up as many as he could find then stuffed them in his mouth.

'Yummy!' screamed Graham.

'Sweets! Where?' chanted the others. Then they stopped to look.

'Over there!' yelled Henry, throwing another handful. The racers paused to pounce on the treats.

While the others munched and crunched, Henry made a frantic dash for the lead.

He was out in front! Henry's legs moved as they had never moved before, pounding round the field. And there was the finishing line!

THUD! THUD! THUD! Henry glanced back. Oh no! Aerobic Al was catching up!

Henry felt in his pocket. He had one giant gob-stopper left. He looked round, panting.

'Go home and take a nap, Henry!' shouted Al, sticking out his tongue as he raced past.

Henry threw down the gob-stopper in front of Al. Aerobic Al hesitated, then skidded to a halt and picked it up. He could beat Henry any day so why not show off a bit?

Suddenly Henry sprinted past. Aerobic Al dashed after him. Harder and harder, faster and faster Henry ran. He was a bird. He was a plane. He flew across the finishing line.

'The winner is … Henry?' squeaked Miss Battle-Axe.

'I've been robbed!' screamed Aerobic Al.

'Hurray!' yelled Henry.

Wow, what a great day, thought Horrid Henry, proudly carrying home his trophy. Al's dad shouting at Miss Battle-Axe and Mum. Miss Battle-Axe and Mum shouting back. Peter sent off in disgrace. And he, Henry, the big winner.

'I can't think how you got those eggs muddled up,' said Mum.

'Me neither,' said Perfect Peter, sniffling.

'Never mind, Peter,' said Henry brightly. 'It's not winning, it's *how* you play that counts.'

HORRID HENRY'S HOMEWORK

Ahhhh, thought Horrid Henry. He turned on the TV and stretched out. School was over. What could be better than lying on the sofa all afternoon, eating crisps and watching TV? Wasn't life grand?

Then Mum came in. She did not look like a mum who thought life was grand. She looked like a mum on the warpath against boys who lay on sofas all afternoon, eating crisps and watching TV.

'Get your feet off the sofa, Henry!' said Mum.

'Unh,' grunted Henry.

'Stop getting crisps everywhere!' snapped Mum.

'Unh,' grunted Henry.

'Have you done your homework, Henry?' said Mum.

Henry didn't answer.

'HENRY!' shouted Mum. $22 + 7 = 49$ X

'WHAT!' shouted Henry.

'Have you done your homework?'

'What homework?' said Henry. He kept his eyes glued to the TV.

'Go, Mutants!' he screeched.

'The five spelling words you are meant to learn tonight,' said Mum.

'Oh,' said Henry. 'That homework.'

Horrid Henry hated homework. He had far better things to do with his precious time than learn how to spell 'zipper' or work out the answer to 6 x 7. For weeks

Henry's homework sheets had ended up in the recycling box until Dad found them. Henry swore he had no idea how they got there and blamed Fluffy the cat, but since then Mum and Dad had checked his school bag every day.

Mum snatched the zapper and switched off the telly.

'Hey, I'm watching!' said Henry.

'When are you going to do your homework, Henry?' said Mum.

'SOON!' screamed Henry. He'd just returned from a long, hard day at school. Couldn't he have any peace around here? When he was king anyone who said the word 'homework' would get thrown to the crocodiles.

'I had a phone call today from Miss Battle-Axe,' said Mum. 'She said you got a zero in the last ten spelling tests.'

'That's not *my* fault,' said Henry. 'First I lost the words, then I forgot, then I couldn't read my writing, then I copied the words wrong, then –'

'I don't want to hear any more silly excuses,' said Mum. 'Do you know your spelling words for tomorrow?'

'Yes,' lied Henry.

'Where's the list?' Mum asked.

'I don't know,' said Henry.

'Find it or no TV for a month,' said Mum.

'It's not fair,' muttered Henry, digging the crumpled spelling list out of his pocket.

Mum looked at it.

'There's going to be a test tomorrow,' she said. 'How do you spell "goat"?'

'Don't you know how, Mum?' asked Henry.

'Henry . . .' said Mum.

Henry scowled.

'I'm busy,' moaned Henry. 'I promise I'll tell you right after Mutant Madman. It's my favourite show.'

'How do you spell "goat"?' said Mum.

'G-O-T-E,' snapped Henry.

'Wrong,' said Mum. 'What about "boat"?'

'Why do I have to do this?' wailed Henry.

'Because it's your homework,' said Mum. 'You have to learn how to spell.'

'But why?' said Henry. 'I never write letters.'

'Because,' said Mum. 'Now spell "boat"'.

'B-O-T-T-E,' said Henry.

'No more TV until you do your homework,' said Mum.

'I've done all *my* homework,' said Perfect Peter. 'In fact I enjoyed it so much I've already done tomorrow's homework as well.'

Henry pounced on Peter. He was a cannibal tenderising his victim for the pot.

'Eeeeyowwww!' screamed Peter.

'Henry! Go to your room!' shouted Mum. 'And don't come out until you know *all* your spelling words!'

Horrid Henry stomped upstairs and slammed his bedroom door. This was so unfair! He was far too busy to bother with stupid, boring, useless spelling. For instance, he hadn't read the new Mutant Madman comic book. He hadn't finished drawing that treasure map. And he hadn't even begun to sort his new collection of Twizzle cards. Homework would have to wait.

There was just one problem. Miss Battle-Axe had said that everyone who spelled all their words correctly tomorrow would get a pack of Big Bopper sweets. Henry loved Big Bopper sweets. Mum and Dad hardly ever let him have them. But why on earth did he have to learn spelling words to get some? If he were the teacher, he'd only give sweets to children who couldn't spell. Henry sighed. He'd just have to sit down and learn those stupid words.

4:30. Mum burst into the room. Henry was lying on his bed reading a comic.

'Henry! Why aren't you doing your homework?' said Mum.

'I'll do it in a sec,' said Henry. 'I'm just finishing this page.'

'Henry ...' said Mum.

Henry put down the comic.

Mum left. Henry picked up the comic.

5.30. Dad burst into the room. Henry was playing with his knights.

'Henry! Why aren't you doing your homework?' said Dad.

'I'm tired!' yawned Henry. 'I'm just taking a little break. It's hard having so much work!'

'Henry, you've only got five words to learn!' said Dad. 'And you've just spent two hours *not* learning them.'

'All right,' snarled Henry. Slowly, he picked up his spelling list. Then he put it down again. He had to get in the mood. Soothing music, that's what he needed. Horrid Henry switched on his cassette player. The terrible sound of the Driller Cannibals boomed through the house.

'OH, I'M A CAN-CAN-CANNIBAL!' screamed Henry, stomping around his room. 'DON'T CALL ME AN ANIMAL JUST 'CAUSE I'M A CAN-CAN-CANNIBAL!'

Mum and Dad stormed into Henry's bedroom and turned off the music.

'That's enough, Henry!' said Dad.

'DO YOUR HOMEWORK!' screamed Mum.

'IF YOU DON'T GET EVERY SINGLE WORD RIGHT IN YOUR TEST TOMORROW THERE WILL BE NO TELEVISION FOR A WEEK!' shouted Dad.

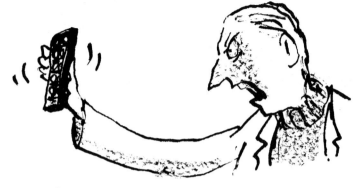

EEEK! No TV *and* no sweets! This was too much. Horrid Henry looked at his spelling words with loathing.

GOAT   BOAT

SAID   STOAT

FRIEND

'I hate goats! I'll never need to spell the word "goat" in my life,' said Henry. He hated goat's cheese. He hated goat's milk. He thought goats were smelly. That was one word he'd definitely never need to know.

The next word was 'boat'. Who needs to spell that, thought Henry. I'm not going to be a sailor when I grow up. I get seasick. In fact, it's bad for my health to learn how to spell 'boat'.

As for 'said', what did it matter if he spelt it 'sed'? It was perfectly understandable, written 'sed.' Only an old fusspot like Miss Battle-Axe would mind such a tiny mistake.

Then there was 'stoat'. What on earth was a stoat? What a mean, sneaky word. Henry wouldn't know a stoat if it sat on him. Of all the useless, horrible words, 'stoat' was the worst. Trust his teacher, Miss Battle-Axe, to make him learn a horrible, useless word like stoat.

The last word was 'friend'. Well, a real friend like Rude Ralph didn't care how the word 'friend' was spelt. As far as Henry was concerned any friend who minded how he spelt 'friend' was no friend. Miss Battle-Axe included that word to torture him.

Five whole spelling words. It was too much. I'll never learn so many words, thought Henry. But what about tomorrow? He'd have to watch Moody Margaret and

Jolly Josh and Clever Clare chomping away at those delicious Big Boppers, while he, Henry, had to gnash his empty teeth. Plus no TV for a week! Henry couldn't live that long without TV! He was sunk. He was doomed to be sweetless, and TV-less.

But wait. What if there was a way to get those sweets without the horrid hassle of learning to spell? Suddenly, Henry had a brilliant, spectacular idea. It was so simple Henry couldn't believe he'd never thought of it before.

He sat next to Clever Clare. Clare always knew the spelling words. All Henry had to do was to take a little peek at her work. If he positioned his chair right, he'd easily be able to see what she wrote. And he wouldn't be copying her, no way. Just double-checking. I am a genius, thought Horrid Henry. 100% right on the test. Loads of Big Bopper sweets. Mum and Dad would be so thrilled they'd let him watch extra TV. Hurray!

Horrid Henry swaggered into class the next morning. He sat down in his seat between Clever Clare and Beefy Bert. Carefully, he inched his chair over a fraction so that he had a good view of Clare's paper.

'Spelling test!' barked Miss Battle-Axe. 'First word – goat.'

Clare bent over her paper. Henry pretended he was staring at the wall, then, quick as a flash, he glanced at her work and wrote 'goat'.

'Boat,' said Miss Battle-Axe. Again Horrid Henry sneaked a look at Clare's paper and copied her. And again. And again.

This is fantastic, thought Henry. I'll never have to learn any spelling words. Just think of all the comic books he could read instead of wasting his time on homework! He sneaked a peek at Beefy Bert's paper. Blank. Ha ha, thought Henry.

There was only one word left. Henry could taste the tingly tang of a Big Bopper already. Wouldn't he swagger about! And no way would he share his sweets with anyone.

Suddenly, Clare shifted position and edged away from him. Rats! Henry couldn't see her paper any more.

'Last word,' boomed Miss Battle-Axe. 'Friend.'

Henry twisted in his seat. He could see the first four words. He just needed to get a tiny bit closer ...

Clare looked at him. Henry stared at the ceiling. Clare glared, then looked back at her paper. Quickly, Henry leaned over and ...YES! He copied down the final word, 'friend'.

Victory!

Chomp! Chomp! Chomp! Hmmnn, boy, did those Big Boppers taste great!

Someone tapped him on the shoulder. It was Miss Battle-Axe. She was smiling at him with her great big yellow teeth. Miss Battle-Axe had never smiled at Henry before.

'Well, Henry,' said Miss Battle-Axe. 'What an improvement! I'm thrilled.'

'Thank you,' said Henry modestly.

'In fact, you've done so well I'm promoting you to the top spelling group. Twenty-five extra words a night. Here's the list.'

Horrid Henry's jaws stopped chomping. He looked

in horror at the new spelling list. It was littered with words. But not just any words. Awful words. Mean words. Long words. HARD words.

Hieroglyphs.

Trapezium.

Diarrhoea.

'AAAAAHHHHHHHHHHH!' shrieked Horrid Henry.

HORRID HENRY'S SPELLING TEST

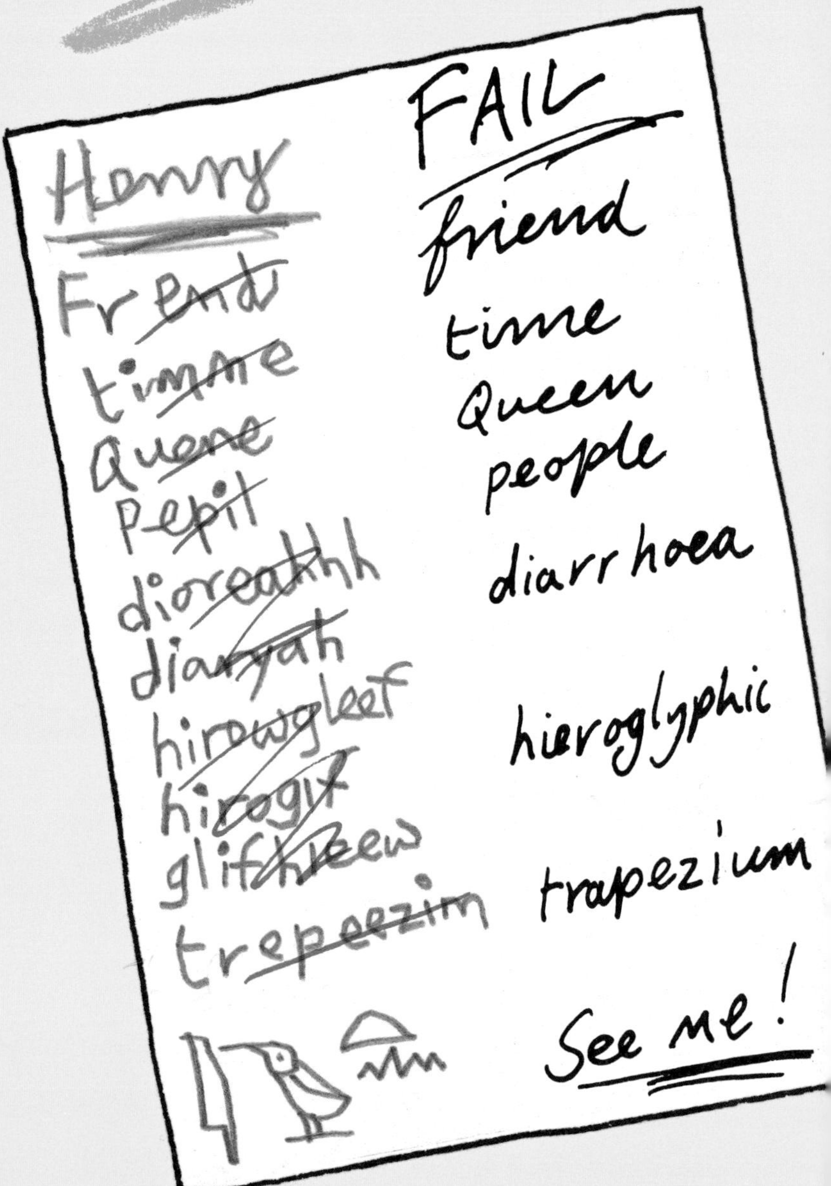

FAIL

Henry

Freud — friend
timare — time
Quene — Queen
P-epit — people
dioreathh
diaryah — diarrhoea
hirowgleet
hirogif — hieroglyphic
glifhkew
trepeezim — trapezium

See me!

HORRID HENRY'S
MATHS TEST

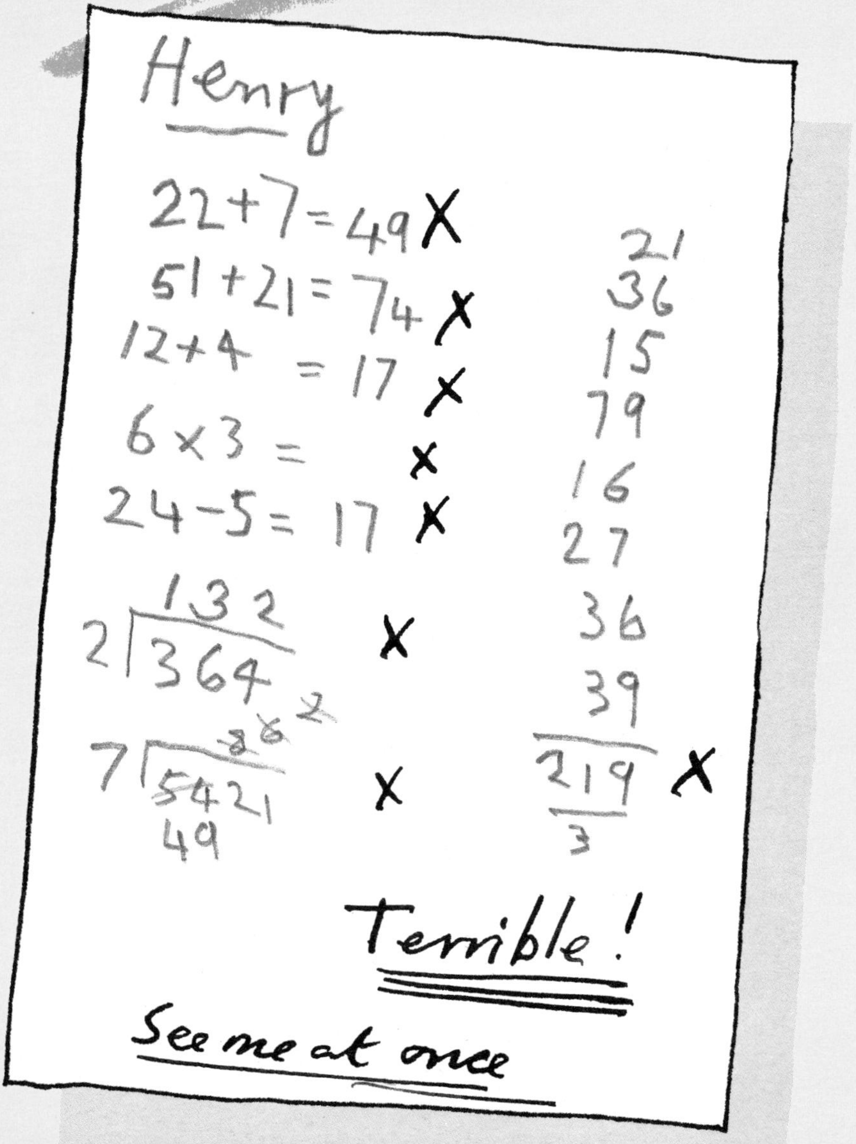

Henry

$22 + 7 = 49$ X   21

$51 + 21 = 74$ X   36

$12 + 4 = 17$ X   15

$6 \times 3 =$ X   79

$24 - 5 = 17$ X   16

                 27

$$2\overline{)364} \;\; \overset{132}{} \quad X \quad 36$$

$$7\overline{)5421} \quad X \quad 39$$
$$49 \qquad\qquad \overline{\underset{3}{219}} \; X$$

Terrible!

See me at once

HORRID HENRY'S SWIMMING LESSON

Oh no! thought Horrid Henry. He pulled the duvet tightly over his head. It was Thursday. Horrible, horrible,  Thursday. The worst day of the week. Horrid Henry was certain Thursdays came more often than any other day. Thursday was his class swimming day. Henry had a nagging feeling that this Thursday was even worse than all the other awful Thursdays.

Horrid Henry liked the bus ride to the pool. Horrid Henry liked doing the dance of the seven towels in the

changing room. He also liked hiding in the lockers, throwing socks in the pool, and splashing everyone.

The only thing Henry didn't like about going swimming was . . . swimming.

The truth was, Horrid Henry hated water. Ugggh! Water was so . . . wet! And soggy. The chlorine stung his eyes. He never knew what horrors might be lurking in the deep end. And the pool was so cold penguins could fly in for the winter.

Fortunately, Henry had a brilliant list of excuses. He'd pretend he had a verucca, or a tummy ache, or had lost his swimming costume. Unfortunately, the mean, nasty, horrible swimming teacher, Soggy Sid, usually made him get in the pool anyway.

Then Henry would duck Dizzy Dave, or splash Weepy William, or pinch Gorgeous Gurinder, until Sid ordered him out. It was not surprising that Horrid Henry had never managed to get his five-metre badge.

Arrrgh! Now he remembered. Today was test day. The terrible day when everyone had to show how far they could swim. Aerobic Al was going for gold. Moody Margaret was going for silver. The only ones who were still trying for their five-metre badges were Lazy Linda and Horrid Henry. Five whole metres! How could anyone swim such a vast distance?

If only they were tested on who could sink to the

bottom of the pool the fastest, or splash the most, or spit water the furthest, then Horrid Henry would have every badge in a jiffy. But no. He had to leap into a freezing cold pool, and, if he survived that shock, somehow thrash his way across five whole metres without drowning.

Well, there was no way he was going to school today.

Mum came into his room.

'I can't go to school today, Mum,' Henry moaned. 'I feel terrible.'

Mum didn't even look at him.

'Thursday-itis again, I presume,' said Mum.

'No way!' said Henry. 'I didn't even know it was Thursday.'

'Get up Henry,' said Mum. 'You're going swimming and that's that.'

Perfect Peter peeked round the door.

'It's badge day today!' he said. 'I'm going for 50 metres!'

'That's brilliant, Peter,' said Mum. 'I bet you're the best swimmer in your class.'

Perfect Peter smiled modestly.

'I just try my best,' he said. 'Good luck with your five-metre badge, Henry,' he added.

Horrid Henry growled and attacked. He was a Venus flytrap slowly mashing a frantic fly between his deadly leaves.

'Eeeeeowwww!' screeched Peter.

'Stop being horrid, Henry!' screamed Mum. 'Leave your poor brother alone!'

Horrid Henry let Peter go. If only he could find some way not to take his swimming test he'd be the happiest boy in the world.

Henry's class arrived at the pool. Right, thought Henry. Time to unpack his excuses to Soggy Sid.

'I can't go swimming, I've got a verucca,' lied Henry.

'Take off your sock,' ordered Soggy Sid.

Rats, thought Henry.

'Maybe it's better now,' said Henry.

'I thought so,' said Sid.

Horrid Henry grabbed his stomach.

'Tummy pains!' he moaned. 'I feel terrible.'

'You seemed fine when you were prancing round the pool a moment ago,' snapped Sid. 'Now get changed.'

Time for the killer excuse.

'I forgot my swimming costume!' said Henry. This was his best chance of success.

'No problem,' said Soggy Sid. He handed Henry a bag. 'Put on one of these.'

Slowly, Horrid Henry rummaged in the bag. He pulled out a bikini top, a blue costume with a hole in the middle, a pair of pink pants, a tiny pair of green trunks, a polka-dot one piece with bunnies, see-through white shorts, and a nappy.

'I can't wear any of these!' protested Horrid Henry.

'You can and you will, if I have to put them on you myself,' snarled Sid.

Horrid Henry squeezed into the green trunks. He could barely breathe. Slowly, he joined the rest of his class pushing and shoving by the side of the pool.

Everyone had millions of badges sewn all over their

costumes. You couldn't even see Aerobic Al's bathing suit beneath the stack of badges.

'Hey you!' shouted Soggy Sid. He pointed at Weepy William. 'Where's your swimming costume?'

Weepy William glanced down and burst into tears.

'Waaaaah,' he wailed, and ran weeping back to the changing room.

'Now get in!' ordered Soggy Sid.

'But I'll drown!' screamed Henry. 'I can't swim!'

'Get in!' screamed Soggy Sid.

Goodbye, cruel world. Horrid Henry held his breath and fell into the icy water. ARRRRGH! He was turning into an iceberg!

He was dying! He was dead! His feet flailed madly as he sank down, down, down – clunk! Henry's feet touched the bottom.

Henry stood up, choking and spluttering. He was waist-deep in water.

'Linda and Henry! Swim five metres – now!'

What am I going to do? thought Henry. It was so humiliating not even being able to swim five metres! Everyone would tease him. And he'd have to listen to them bragging about their badges! Wouldn't it be great to get a badge? Somehow?

Lazy Linda set off, very very slowly. Horrid Henry grabbed on to her leg. Maybe she'll pull me across, he thought.

'Ugggh!' gurgled Lazy Linda.

'Leave her alone!' shouted Sid. 'Last chance, Henry.'

Horrid Henry ran along the pool's bottom and flapped his arms, pretending to swim.

'Did it!' said Henry.

Soggy Sid scowled.

'I said swim, not walk!' screamed Sid. 'You've failed. Now get over to the far lane and practise. Remember, anyone who stops swimming during the test doesn't get a badge.'

Horrid Henry stomped over to the far lane. No way was he going to practise! How he hated swimming! He watched the others splashing up and down, up and down. There was Aerobic Al, doing his laps like a bolt of

lightning. And Moody Margaret. And Kung-Fu Kate.
Everyone would be getting a badge but Henry. It was
so unfair.

'Pssst, Susan,' said Henry. 'Have you heard? There's a
shark in the deep end!'

'Oh yeah, right,' said Sour Susan. She looked at the
dark water in the far end of the pool.

'Don't believe me,' said Henry. 'Find out the hard
way. Come back with a leg missing.'

Sour Susan paused and whispered something to
Moody Margaret.

'Shut up, Henry,' said Margaret. They swam off.

'Don't worry about the shark, Andrew,' said Henry. 'I
think he's already eaten today.'

'What shark?' said Anxious Andrew.

Andrew stared at the deep end. It did look awfully dark down there.

'Start swimming, Andrew!' shouted Soggy Sid.

'I don't want to,' said Andrew.

'Swim! Or I'll bite you myself!' snarled Sid.

Andrew started swimming.

'Dave, Ralph, Clare, and Bert – start swimming!' bellowed Soggy Sid.

'Look out for the shark!' said Horrid Henry. He watched Aerobic Al tearing up and down the lane. 'Gotta swim, gotta swim, gotta swim,' muttered Al between strokes.

What a show-off, thought Henry. Wouldn't it be fun to play a trick on him?

Horrid Henry pretended he was a crocodile. He sneaked under the water to the middle of the pool and waited until Aerobic Al swam overhead. Then Horrid Henry reached up.

Pinch! Henry grabbed Al's thrashing leg.

'AAAARGGG!' screamed Al. 'Something's grabbed my leg. Help!' Aerobic Al leaped out of the pool.

Tee hee, thought Horrid Henry.

'It's a shark!' screamed Sour Susan. She scrambled out of the pool.

'There's a shark in the pool!' screeched Anxious Andrew.

'There's a shark in the pool!' howled Rude Ralph.

Everyone was screaming and shouting and struggling to get out.

The only one left in the pool was Henry.

Shark!

Horrid Henry forgot there were no sharks in swimming pools.

Horrid Henry forgot he'd started the shark rumour.

Horrid Henry forgot he couldn't swim.

All he knew was that he was alone in the pool – with a shark!

Horrid Henry swam for his life. Shaking and quaking, splashing and crashing, he torpedoed his way to the side of the pool and scrambled out. He gasped and panted. Thank goodness. Safe at last! He'd never ever go swimming again.

'Five metres!' bellowed Soggy Sid. 'You've all failed your badges today, except for – Henry!'

'Waaaaaaahhhhhh!' wailed the other children.

'Whoopee!' screamed Henry. 'Olympics, here I come!'

HORRID HENRY
AND THE
DEMON DINNER LADY

'You're not having a packed lunch and that's final,' yelled Dad.

'It's not fair!' yelled Horrid Henry. 'Everyone in my class has a packed lunch.'

'N-O spells no,' said Dad. 'It's too much work. And you never eat what I pack for you.'

'But I hate school dinners!' screamed Henry. 'I'm being poisoned!' He clutched his throat. 'Dessert today was – bleeeach – fruit salad! And it had worms in it! I can feel them slithering in my stomach – uggghh!' Horrid Henry fell to the floor, gasping and rasping.

Mum continued watching TV.

Dad continued watching TV.

'I love school dinners,' said Perfect Peter. 'They're so nutritious and delicious. Especially those lovely spinach salads.'

'Shut up, Peter!' snarled Henry.

'Muuuum!' wailed Peter. 'Henry told me to shut up!'

'Don't be horrid, Henry!' said Mum. 'You're not having a packed lunch and that's that.'

Horrid Henry and his parents had been fighting about packed lunches for weeks. Henry was desperate to have a packed lunch. Actually, he was desperate not to have a school dinner.

Horrid Henry hated school dinners. The stinky smell. The terrible way Sloppy Sally ladled the food *splat*! on his tray so that most of it splashed all over him. And the food! Queueing for hours for revolting ravioli and squashed tomatoes. The lumpy custard. The blobby mashed potatoes. Horrid Henry could not bear it any longer.

'Oh please,' said Henry. 'I'll make the packed lunch myself.' Wouldn't that be great! He'd fill his lunchbox with four packs of crisps, chocolate, doughnuts, cake, lollies, and one grape. Now that's what I call a real lunch, thought Henry.

Mum sighed.

Dad sighed.

They looked at each other.

'If you promise that everything in your lunchbox will get eaten, then I'll do a packed lunch for you,' said Dad.

'Oh thank you thank you thank you!' said Horrid Henry. 'Everything will get eaten, I promise.' Just not by me, he thought gleefully. Packed lunch room, here I come. Food fights, food swaps, food fun at last. Yippee!

Horrid Henry strolled into the packed lunch room. He was King Henry the Horrible, surveying his unruly subjects. All around him children were screaming and

shouting, pushing and shoving, throwing food and trading treats. Heaven! Horrid Henry smiled happily and opened his Terminator Gladiator lunchbox.

Hmmn. An egg salad sandwich. On brown bread. With crusts. Yuck! But he could always swap it for one of Greedy Graham's stack of chocolate spread sandwiches. Or one of Rude Ralph's jam rolls. That was the great thing about packed lunches, thought Henry. Someone always wanted what you had. No one *ever* wanted someone else's school dinner. Henry shuddered.

But those bad days were behind him, part of the dim and distant past. A horror story to tell his grand-children. Henry could see it now. A row of horrified toddlers, screaming and crying while he told terrifying tales of stringy stew and soggy semolina.

Now, what else? Henry's fingers closed on something round. An apple. Great, thought Henry, he could use it for target practice, and the carrots would be perfect for poking Gorgeous Gurinder when she wasn't looking.

Henry dug deeper. What was buried right at the

bottom? What was hidden under the celery sticks and the granola bar? Oh boy! Crisps! Henry loved crisps. So salty! So crunchy! So yummy! His mean, horrible parents only let him have crisps once a week. Crisps! What bliss! He could taste their delicious saltiness already. He wouldn't share them with anyone, no matter how hard they begged. Henry tore open the bag and reached in –

Suddenly a huge shadow fell over him. A fat greasy hand shot out. Snatch! Crunch. Crunch.

Horrid Henry's crisps were gone.

Henry was so shocked that for a moment he could not speak. 'Wha–wha–what was that?' gasped Henry as a gigantic woman waddled between the tables. 'She just stole my crisps!'

'That,' said Rude Ralph grimly, 'was Greta. She's the demon dinner lady.'

'Watch out for her!' squealed Sour Susan.

'She's the sneakiest snatcher in school,' wailed Weepy William.

What? A dinner lady who snatched food instead of dumping it on your plate? How could this be? Henry stared as Greasy Greta patrolled up and down the aisles. Her piggy eyes darted from side to side. She ignored Aerobic Al's carrots. She ignored Tidy Ted's yoghurt.

She ignored Goody-Goody Gordon's orange.

Then suddenly –

Snatch! Chomp. Chomp. Sour Susan's sweets were gone.

Snatch! Chomp. Chomp. Dizzy Dave's doughnut was gone.

Snatch! Chomp. Chomp. Beefy Bert's biscuits were gone.

Moody Margaret looked up from her lunch.

'Don't look up!' shrieked Susan. Too late! Greasy Greta swept Margaret's food away, stuffing Margaret's uneaten chocolate bar into her fat wobbly cheeks.

'Hey, I wasn't finished!' screamed Margaret. Greasy Greta ignored her and marched on. Weepy William tried to hide his toffees under his cheese sandwich. But Greasy Greta wasn't fooled.

Snatch! Gobble. Gobble. The toffees vanished down Greta's gaping gob.

'Waaah,' wailed William. 'I want my toffees!'

'No sweets in school,' barked Greasy Greta. She marched up and down, up and down, snatching and grabbing, looting and devouring, wobbling and gobbling.

Why had no one told him there was a demon dinner lady in charge of the packed lunch room?

'Why didn't you warn me about her, Ralph?' demanded Henry.

Rude Ralph shrugged. 'It wouldn't have done any good. She is unstoppable.'

We'll see about that, thought Henry. He glared at Greta. No way would Greasy Greta grab his food again.

On Tuesday Greta snatched Henry's doughnut.

On Wednesday Greta snatched Henry's cake.

On Thursday Greta snatched Henry's biscuits.

On Friday, as usual, Horrid Henry persuaded Anxious Andrew to swap his crisps for Henry's granola bar. He persuaded Kung-Fu Kate to swap her chocolates for Henry's raisins. He persuaded Beefy Bert to swap his biscuits for Henry's carrots. But what was the use of being a brilliant food trader, thought Henry miserably, if Greasy Greta just swooped and snaffled his hard-won treats?

Henry tried hiding his desserts. He tried eating his desserts secretly. He tried tugging them back. But it was no use. The moment he snapped open his lunchbox – SNATCH! Greasy Greta grabbed the goodies.

Something had to be done.

'Mum,' complained Henry, 'there's a demon dinner lady at school snatching our sweets.'

'That's nice, Henry,' said Mum, reading her newspaper.

'Dad,' complained Henry, 'there's a demon dinner lady at school snatching our sweets.'

'Good,' said Dad. 'You eat too many sweets.'

'We're not allowed to bring sweets to school, Henry,' said Perfect Peter.

'But it's not fair!' squealed Henry. 'She takes crisps, too.'

'If you don't like it, go back to school dinners,' said Dad.

'No!' howled Henry. 'I hate school dinners!' Watery gravy with bits. Lumpy surprise with lumps. Gristly glop with globules. Food with its own life slopping

about on his tray. NO! Horrid Henry couldn't face it. He'd fought so hard for a packed lunch. Even a packed lunch like the one Dad made, fortified with eight essential minerals and vitamins, was better than going back to school dinners.

He could, of course, just eat healthy foods. Greta never snatched those. Henry imagined his lunchbox, groaning with alfalfa sprouts on wholemeal brown bread studded with chewy bits. Ugh! Bleeeach! Torture!

He had to keep his packed lunch. But he had to stop Greta. He just had to.

And then suddenly Henry had a brilliant, spectacular idea. It was so brilliant that for a moment he could hardly believe he'd thought of it. Oh boy, Greta, thought Henry gleefully, are you going to be sorry you messed with me.

Lunchtime. Horrid Henry sat with his lunchbox unopened. Rude Ralph was armed and ready beside him. Now, where was Greta?

Thump. Thump. Thump. The floor shook as the demon dinner lady started her food patrol. Horrid Henry waited until she was almost behind him. SNAP!

He opened his lunchbox.

SNATCH! The familiar greasy hand shot out, grabbed Henry's biscuits and shovelled them into her mouth. Her terrible teeth began to chomp.

And then –

'Yiaowwww! Aaaarrrgh!' A terrible scream echoed through the packed lunch room.

Greasy Greta turned purple. Then pink. Then bright red.

'Yiaowwww!' she howled. 'I need to cool down!
Gimme that!' she screeched, snatching Rude Ralph's
doughnut and stuffing it in her mouth.

'Aaaarrrgh!' she choked. 'I'm on fire! Water! Water!'

She grabbed a pitcher of water, poured it on top of
herself, then ran howling down the aisle and out the
door.

For a moment there was silence. Then the entire
packed lunch room started clapping and cheering.

'Wow, Henry,' said Greedy Graham, 'what did you
do to her?'

'Nothing,' said Horrid Henry. 'She just tried my
special recipe. Hot chilli powder biscuits, anyone?'

Bert, what's for lunch?

I dunno

what's on telly tonight?

Hog House

Yippee!

HORRID HENRY
READS A BOOK

Blah blah blah blah blah.

Miss Battle-Axe droned on and on and on.

Horrid Henry drew pictures of crocodiles tucking into a juicy Battle-Axe snack in his maths book.

Snap! Off went her head.

Yank! Bye bye leg.

Crunch! Ta-ta teeth.

Yum yum. Henry's crocodile had a big fat smile on its face.

Blah blah blah books blah blah blah read blah blah blah prize blah blah

...PRIZE?

Horrid Henry stopped doodling.

'What prize?' he shrieked.

'Don't shout out, Henry,' said Miss Battle-Axe.

Horrid Henry waved his hand and shouted:

'What prize?'

'Well, Henry, if you'd been paying attention instead of scribbling, you'd know, wouldn't you?' said Miss Battle-Axe.

Horrid Henry scowled. Typical teacher. You're interested enough in what they're saying to ask a question, and suddenly they don't want to answer.

'So class, as I was saying before I was so rudely interrupted –' she glared at Horrid Henry – 'you'll have two weeks to read as many books as you can for our school reading competition. Whoever reads the most

114

books will win an exciting prize. A very exciting prize. But remember, a book report on every book on your list, please.'

Oh. A reading competition. Horrid Henry slumped in his chair. Phooey. Reading was hard, heavy work. Just turning the pages made Henry feel exhausted. Why couldn't they ever do fun competitions, like whose tummy could rumble the loudest, or who shouted out the most in class, or who knew the rudest words? Horrid Henry would win *those* competitions every time.

But no. Miss Battle-Axe would never have a *fun* competition. Well, no way was he taking part in a reading contest. Henry would just have to watch some-one undeserving like Clever Clare or Brainy Brian swagger off with the prize while he sat prize-less at the back. It was so unfair!

'What's the prize?' shouted Moody Margaret.

Probably something awful like a pencil case, thought Horrid Henry. Or a bumper pack of school tea towels.

'Sweets!' shouted Greedy Graham.

'A million pounds!' shouted Rude Ralph.

'Clothes!' shouted Gorgeous Gurinder.

'A skateboard!' shouted Aerobic Al.

'A hamster!' said Anxious Andrew.

'Silence!' bellowed Miss Battle-Axe. 'The prize is a family ticket to a brand new theme park.'

Horrid Henry sat up. A theme park! Oh wow! He loved theme parks! Rollercoasters! Water rides! Candy floss! His mean, horrible parents never took him to theme parks. They dragged him to museums. They hauled him on hikes. But if he won the competition, they'd have to take him. He had to win that prize. He had to. But how could he win a reading competition without reading any books?

'Do comics count?' shouted Rude Ralph.

Horrid Henry's heart leapt. He was king of the comic book readers. He'd easily win a comic book competition.

Miss Battle-Axe glared at Ralph with her beady eyes.

'Of course not!' she said. 'Clare! How many books do you think you can read?'

'Fifteen,' said Clever Clare.

'Brian?'

'Eighteen,' said Brainy Brian.

'Nineteen,' said Clare.

'Twenty,' said Brian.

Horrid Henry smiled. Wouldn't they get a shock when he won the prize? He'd start reading the second he got home.

Horrid Henry stretched out in the comfy black chair

and switched on the TV. He had plenty of time to read. He'd start tomorrow.

Tuesday. Oh boy! Five new comics! He'd read them first and start on all those books later.

Wednesday. Whoopee! A Mutant Max TV special! He'd definitely get reading afterwards.

Thursday. Rude Ralph brought round his great new computer game, 'Mash 'em! Smash 'em!' Henry mashed and smashed and mashed and smashed . . .

Friday. Yawn. Horrid Henry was exhausted after his long, hard week. I'll read tons of books tomorrow, thought Henry. After all, there was loads of time till the competition ended.

'How many books have you read, Henry?' asked Perfect Peter, looking up from the sofa.

'Loads,' lied Henry.

'I've read five,' said Perfect Peter proudly. 'More than anyone in my class.'

'Goody for you,' said Henry.

'You're just jealous,' said Peter.

'As if I'd ever be jealous of you, worm,' sneered Henry. He wandered over to the sofa. 'So what are you reading?'

'*The Happy Nappy*,' said Peter.

The Happy Nappy! Trust Peter to read a stupid book like that.

'What's it about?' asked Henry, snorting.

'It's great,' said Peter. 'It's all about this nappy –' Then he stopped. 'Wait, I'm not telling *you*. You just want to find out so you can use it in the competition. Well, you're too late. Tomorrow is the last day.'

Horrid Henry felt as if a dagger had been plunged into his heart. This couldn't be. Tomorrow! How had tomorrow sneaked up so fast?

'What!' shrieked Henry. 'The competition ends – tomorrow?'

'Yes,' said Peter. 'You should have started reading sooner. After all, why put off till tomorrow what you can do today?'

'Shut up!' said Horrid Henry. He looked around wildly. What to do, what to do. He had to read something, anything – fast.

'Gimme that!' snarled Henry, snatching Peter's book. Frantically, he started to read:

'I'm unhappy, pappy,' said the snappy nappy. 'A happy nappy is a clappy –'

Perfect Peter snatched back his book.

'No!' screamed Peter, holding on tightly. 'It's mine.'

Henry lunged.

'Mine!'

'Mine!'

Riii—iippp.

'MUUUUMMMM!' screamed Peter. 'Henry tore my book!'

Mum and Dad ran into the room.

'You're fighting—over a book?' said Mum. She sat down in a chair.

'I'm speechless,' said Mum.

'Well, I'm not,' said Dad. 'Henry! Go to your room!'

'Fine!' screamed Horrid Henry.

Horrid Henry prowled up and down his bedroom. He had to think of something. Fast.

Aha! The room was full of books. He'd just copy down lots of titles. Phew. Easy-peasy.

And then suddenly Horrid Henry remembered. He had to write a book report for every book he read. Rats. Miss Battle-Axe knew loads and loads of books. She was sure to know the plot of *Jack the Kangaroo* or *The Adventures of Terry the Tea Towel*.

Well, he'd just have to borrow Peter's list.

Horrid Henry sneaked into Peter's bedroom. There was Peter's competition entry, in the centre of Peter's immaculate desk. Henry read it.

Of course Peter would have the boring and horrible
Mouse Goes to Town. Could he live with the shame of
having baby books like *The Happy Nappy* and *Mouse
Goes to Town* on his competition entry?

For a day at a theme park, anything.

Quickly, Henry copied Peter's list and book reports.
Whoopee! Now he had five books. Wheel of Death
here I come, thought Horrid Henry.

Then Henry had to face the terrible truth. Peter's
books wouldn't be enough to win. He'd heard Clever
Clare had seventeen. If only he didn't have to write
those book reports. Why oh why did Miss Battle-Axe
have to know every book ever written?

And then suddenly Henry had a brilliant, spectacular
idea. It was so brilliant, and so simple, that Horrid
Henry was amazed. Of course there were books that
Miss Battle-Axe didn't know. Books that hadn't been
written – yet.

Horrid Henry grabbed his list.

'*Mouse Goes to Town*. The thrilling adventures of a
mouse in town. He meets a dog, a cat, and a duck.'

Why should that poor mouse just go to town? Quickly Henry began to scribble.

'*Mouse Goes to the Country*. The thrilling adventures of a mouse in the country. He meets –'

Henry paused. What sort of things did you meet in the country? Henry had no idea.

Aha. Henry wrote quickly. 'He meets a sheep and a werewolf.'

'*Mouse Goes Round the World*. Mouse discovers that the world is round.'

'*Mouse Goes to the Loo*. The thrilling adventures of one mouse and his potty.'

Now, perhaps, something a little different. How about *A Boy and his Pig*. What could that book be about? thought Henry.

'Once upon a time there was a boy and his pig. They played together every day. The pig went oink.'

Sounds good to me, thought Henry.

Then there was *A Pig and his Boy.* And, of course, *A Boyish Pig. A Piggish Boy. Two Pigs and a Boy. Two Boys and a Pig.*

Horrid Henry wrote and wrote and wrote. When he had filled up four pages with books and reports, and his hand ached from writing, he stopped and counted.

Twenty-seven books! Surely that was more than enough!

Miss Battle-Axe rose from her seat and walked to the podium in the school hall. Horrid Henry was so excited he could scarcely breathe. He had to win. He was sure to win.

'Well done, everyone,' said Miss Battle-Axe. 'So many wonderful books read. But sadly, there can be only one winner.'

Me! thought Horrid Henry.

'The winner of the school reading competition, the winner who will be receiving a fabulous prize, is –' Horrid Henry got ready to leap up – 'Clare, with twenty-eight books!'

Horrid Henry sank back down in his seat as Clever Clare swaggered up to the podium. If only he'd added *Three Boys, Two Pigs, and a Rhinoceros* to his list, he'd have tied for first. It was so unfair. All his hard work for nothing.

'Well done, Clare!' beamed Miss Battle-Axe. She waved Clare's list. 'I see you've read one of my very favourites, *Boudicca's Big Battle*.'

She stopped. 'Oh dear. Clare, you've put down *Boudicca's Big Battle* twice by mistake. But never mind. I'm sure no one else has read *twenty-seven* books –'

'I have!' screamed Horrid Henry. Leaping and shouting, punching the air with his fist,

Horrid Henry ran up onto the stage, chanting: 'Theme park! Theme park! Theme park!'

'Gimme my prize!' he screeched, snatching the tickets out of Clare's hand.

'Mine!' screamed Clare, snatching them back.

Miss Battle-Axe looked grim. She scanned Henry's list.

'I am not familiar with the *Boy and Pig* series,' she said.

'That's 'cause it's Australian,' said Horrid Henry.

Miss Battle-Axe glared at him. Then she tried to twist her face into a smile.

'It appears we have a tie,' she said. 'Therefore, you will each receive a family pass to the new theme park, Book World. Congratulations.'

Horrid Henry stopped his victory dance. Book World? Book World? Surely he'd heard wrong?

'Here are just some of the wonderful attractions you will enjoy at Book World,' said Miss Battle-Axe. ' 'Thrill to a display of speed-reading! Practice checking out library books! Read to the beat! Oh my, doesn't that sound fun!'

'AAAAAARGGGGGGGGG!' screamed Horrid Henry.

HORRID HENRY'S SCHOOL PROJECT

'**S**usan! Stop shouting!

Ralph! Stop running!

William! Stop weeping!

Henry! Just stop!'

Miss Battle-Axe glared at her class. Her class glared back.

'Miss!' screeched Lazy Linda. 'Henry's pulling my hair.'

'Miss!' screeched Gorgeous Gurinder. 'Ralph's kicking me.'

'Miss!' screeched Anxious Andrew. 'Dave's poking me.'

'Stop it, Henry!' barked Miss Battle-Axe.

Henry stopped. What was bothering the old bat now?

'Class, pay attention,' said Miss Battle-Axe. 'Today we're doing Group Projects on the Ancient Greeks. We're studying –'

'– the sacking of Troy!' shrieked Henry. Yes! He could see it now. Henry, leading the Greeks as they crashed and slashed their way through the terrified Trojans. His spear would be the longest, and the sharpest, and –

Miss Battle-Axe fixed Henry with her icy stare. Henry froze.

'We're going to divide into small groups and make Parthenons out of cardboard loo rolls and card,' continued Miss Battle-Axe. 'First you must draw the Parthenon, agree a design together, then build and paint it. I want to see *everyone* sharing and listening. Also, the Head Teacher will be dropping by to admire your work and to see how beautifully you are working together.'

Horrid Henry scowled. He hated working in groups. He detested sharing. He loathed listening to others. Their ideas were always wrong. His ideas were always right. But the other children in Henry's groups never recognised Henry's genius. For some reason they wanted to do things *their* way, not his.

The Ancient Greeks certainly never worked together beautifully, thought Horrid Henry resentfully, so why should he? They just speared each other or ate their children for tea.

'Henry, Bert, William, and Clare, you're working together on Table Three,' said Miss Battle-Axe.

Horrid Henry groaned. What a horrible, horrible group. He hated all of them. Why did Miss Battle-Axe never put him in a fun group, with Ralph or Graham or Dave? Henry could see it now. They'd be laughing together in the corner, making trumpets out of loo rolls, sneaking sweets, throwing crayons, flicking paint, having a great time.

But oh no. He had to be with bossyboots Clare, crybaby William and – Bert. Miss Battle-Axe did it on purpose, just to torture him.

'NO!' protested Horrid Henry. 'I can't work with *her!*'

'NO!' protested Clever Clare. 'I can't work with *him!*'

'Waaaaah,' wailed Weepy William. 'I want to work with Andrew.'

'Silence!' shouted Miss Battle-Axe. 'Now get in your groups and get to work. I want to see everyone sharing and working together beautifully – or else.'

There was a mad scramble as everyone ran to their tables to grab the best pencils and the most pieces of paper.

Henry snatched the purple, blue and red pencils and a big pile of paper.

'I haven't got any paper!' screamed William.

'Tough,' said Horrid Henry. 'I need all these for my design.'

'I want some paper!' whined William.

Clever Clare passed him one of her sheets.

William burst into tears.

'It's dirty,' he wailed. 'And I haven't got a pencil.'

'Here's what we're going to do,' said Henry. 'I'm doing the design, William can help me build it, and everyone can watch me paint.'

'No way, Henry,' said Clare. 'We *all* do a design, then we make the best one.'

'Which will be mine,' said Horrid Henry.

'Doubt it,' said Clever Clare.

'Well I'm not making *yours*,' snarled Henry. 'And *I'm* doing the painting.'

'You're doing the glueing, *I'm* doing the painting,' said Clare.

'I want to do the painting,' wailed William.

'What do you want to do, Bert?' asked Clare.

'I dunno,' said Beefy Bert.

'Fine,' said Clever Clare. 'Bert will do the tidying. Let's get drawing, everyone. We want our group's Parthenon to be the best.'

Horrid Henry was outraged.

'Who made you boss?' demanded Henry.

'Someone has to take charge,' said Clever Clare.

Horrid Henry reached under the table and kicked her.

'OOWWWW!' yelped Clever Clare. 'Miss! Henry kicked me!'

'Did not!' shouted Horrid Henry. 'Liar.'

'Why isn't Table Three drawing?' hissed Miss Battle-Axe.

Clare drew.

William drew.

Bert drew.

Henry drew.

'Everyone should have finished drawing by now,' said Miss Battle-Axe, patrolling among the tables. 'Time to combine your ideas.'

'But I haven't finished,' wept William.

Horrid Henry gazed at his design with satisfaction. It was a triumph. He could see it now, painted silver and purple, with a few red stripes.

'Why don't we just build mine?' said Clare.

''Cos mine's the best!' shouted Horrid Henry.

'What about mine?' whispered William.

'We're building mine!' shouted Clare.

'MINE!'

'MINE!'

Miss Battle-Axe ran over.

'Stop shouting!' shouted Miss Battle-Axe. 'Show me your work. That's lovely, Clare. What a fabulous design.'

'Thank you, miss,' said Clever Clare.

'William! That's a tower, not a temple! Start again!'

'Waaaah!' wailed William.

'Bert! What is this mess?'

'I dunno,' said Beefy Bert.

'It looks like a teepee, not a temple,' said Miss Battle-Axe.

She looked at Horrid Henry's design and glared at him.

'Can't you follow instructions?' she shrieked. 'That temple looks like it's about to blast off.'

'That's how I meant it to look,' said Henry. 'It's high-tech.'

'Margaret! Sit down! Toby! Leave Brian alone! Graham! Get back to work,' said Miss Battle-Axe, racing off to stop the fight on Table Two.

'Right, we're doing *my* design,' said Clare. 'Who wants to build the steps and who wants to decorate the columns?'

'No one,' snapped Horrid Henry, ''cos we're doing *mine.*'

'Fine, we'll vote,' said Clare. 'Who wants to build mine?'

Clare and William raised their hands.

'I'll get you for that, William,' muttered Henry.

William burst into tears.

'Who wants to do Henry's?' said Clare.

Only Henry raised his hand.

'Come on Bert, don't you want to make mine?' pleaded Henry.

'I dunno,' said Beefy Bert.

'It's not fair!' shrieked Horrid Henry. 'I WANT TO BUILD MINE!'

'MINE!'

'MINE!'

'SLAP!'

'SLAP!

'That's it!' shrieked Miss Battle-Axe. 'Henry! Work in the corner on your own.'

YES! This was the best news Henry had heard all morning.

Beaming, Henry went to the corner and sat down at his own little table, with his own glue, his own scissors, his own paints, his own card, and his own pile of loo rolls.

Bliss, thought Henry. I can build my Parthenon in peace.

There was just one problem. There was only a small number of loo rolls left.

This isn't nearly enough for my Parthenon, thought Horrid Henry. I need more.

He went over to Moody Margaret's table.

'I need more loo rolls,' he said.

'Tough,' said Margaret, 'we're using all of ours.'

Henry stomped over to Sour Susan's table.

'Give me some loo rolls,' he said.

'Go away,' said Susan sourly. 'Margaret took our extras.'

'Sit down, Henry,' barked Miss Battle-Axe.

Henry sat, fuming. This was an outrage. Hadn't Miss Battle-Axe told them to share? And here were his greedy classmates hogging all the loo rolls when his Parthenon desperately needed extra engines.

BUZZZ. Breaktime!

'Leave your Parthenons on the tables to dry,' said Miss Battle-Axe. 'Henry, you will stay in at break and finish.'

What?

Miss break?

'But – but –'

'Sit down,' ordered Miss Battle-Axe. 'Or you'll go straight to the Head!'

Eeeek! Horrid Henry knew the Head, Mrs Oddbod, all too well. He did not need to know her any better.

Henry slunk back to his chair. Everyone else ran shrieking out of the door to the playground. Why was it always children who were punished? Why weren't teachers ever sent to the Head? It was so unfair!

'I just have to nip down the hall for a moment. Don't you dare leave that table,' said Miss Battle-Axe.

The moment Miss Battle-Axe left the room, Henry jumped up and accidentally on purpose knocked over Clare's chair. He broke William's pencil and drew a skull and crossbones on Bert's teepee.

Then he wandered over to Sour Susan's table. There was a freshly-glued Parthenon, waiting to be painted.

Henry studied it.

You know, he thought, Susan's group hasn't done a bad job. Not bad at all. Shame about that bulge on the side, though. If they shared one loo roll with me, it would balance so much better.

Horrid Henry looked to the left.

He looked to the right.

Snatch! Susan's supports sagged.

Better even that up, thought Horrid Henry.

Yank!

Hmmn, thought Horrid Henry,  glancing at Gurinder's table. What were they thinking?

Those walls are far too tall.

Grab! Gurinder's temple tottered.

And as for Clare's pathetic efforts, it was positively bursting with useless pillars.

Whisk! Clare's columns wobbled.

Much better, thought Horrid Henry. Soon he had plenty of loo rolls.

CLOMP

CLOMP

CLOMP

Horrid Henry dashed back to his table and was innocently glueing away as the class stampeded back to their tables.

Wobble

Wobble

Wobble – CRASH!

On every table, Parthenons started collapsing.

Everyone shrieked and screamed and sobbed.

'It's your fault!'

'Yours!'

'You didn't glue it right!'

'You didn't build it right!'

Rude Ralph hurled a paintbrush at Moody Margaret. Margaret hurled it back. Suddenly the room was filled with flying brushes, gluepots and loo rolls.

Miss Battle-Axe burst in.

'STOP IT!' bellowed Miss Battle-Axe, as a loo roll hit her on the nose. 'YOU ARE THE WORST CLASS I HAVE EVER TAUGHT! I LEAVE YOU ALONE FOR ONE MINUTE AND JUST LOOK AT THIS MESS! NOW SIT DOWN AND SHUT –'

The door opened. In walked the Head.

Mrs Oddbod stared at Miss Battle-Axe.

Miss Battle-Axe stared at Mrs Oddbod.

'Boudicca!' said Mrs Oddbod. 'What-is-going-on?'

'The sacking of Troy!' shrieked Horrid Henry.

There was a terrible silence.

Horrid Henry shrank in his seat. Now he was done for. Now he was dead.

'I can see that,' said Mrs Oddbod coldly. 'Miss Battle-Axe! Come to my office – now!'

'No!' whimpered Miss Battle-Axe.

YES! thought Horrid Henry.

Victory!